MW00893775

ISBN (Paperback): 979-8-9874996-9-6
ISBN (eBook): 979-8-9878693-0-7

This book is dedicated to my two babies,
who can fly whenever they want to.

Love,

Mom

Thank you to the One who gave me wings.

Rolly the earthworm and his best friend, Susy,
a ladybug, were playing out in the field when
they saw something hanging from a tree.

It was a cocoon. Suddenly,
a colorful butterfly popped out.

Both said "aww" and watched it fly away.

That night Rolly told his parents,
"I want to fly."

His father said, "No, No; we must stay close to
the ground and away from the birds,
or they will eat you."

The little earthworm went to his room sad.

He did not want to live in the ground forever,
and flying looked fun.

When Rolly was in bed, he saw something glowing outside his window. It was a firefly shining lights.

He fell asleep and had a dream about flying in the clouds.

He was very excited.

Rolly told Susy about his dream of flying.

While the worm was thinking, the ladybug spread her wings and flew over him, thinking too.

HMM...How will they get him off the ground and into the sky?

Larry, the bumble bee, was buzzing by when he saw Rolly with a sad face and asked what was wrong.

The worm said, "I want to be like you and fly."

Then the bumble bee sat down on a flower, looked at him, and said, "Worms don't fly."

Fiona, the dragonfly, was flying by. "You want to do something you are not made to do. Worms must stay in the dirt," she said.

Then they flew off.

Susy had a bright idea. "We should go to the wise spider. I bet he can help. He can make wings for you. I am not giving up on you Rolly," she said.

They went to the spider's house and asked him for help.

The old spider smiled, and helped them.

The spider spun some webs around Rolly and tied leaves to his back.

Tada...he had a pair of wings!

Rolly was so excited to try out the wings.

He climbed up the side of a tree but did not go high.

He pushed himself away and
came crashing down hard on the dirt.

Plop!

On top of the tree was a bird's nest;
the mother bird was watching Rolly.

He could be food for her babies.
When she saw that he had something green on his
back, she did not want to catch him.

Then, she watched Rolly climb up the
tree again and fall.

Plop!

The wings and spider webs got broken
when Rolly fell.

"Ouchy," said Susy.

On the way home, Rolly and
Susy met a caterpillar named Pauly.

The caterpillar asked the worm why he was sad.
Rolly said, "I want wings."

The caterpillar said, "I have to go away for a little
bit, but when I come back; I will be a butterfly."

This made Rolly and Susy think.
They remembered the cocoon hanging from the tree. "So, that's how wings are made."

They returned to the wise spider and asked him to make them a cocoon.

The spider smiled and helped them.

The mother bird sees Rolly again,
but he is inside a cocoon.

She looks at him and wonders why he is in there.

Rolly's parents found him hanging in a
cocoon on a tree.

He told them, "I am growing wings. Yay!"

But he did not grow wings because
he was not a caterpillar.

Rolly would not give up. He would keep trying to fly
because he wanted to be in the air, not in the dirt.

Others in the wood thought Rolly was funny because he wanted to be different.

They got together to talk about him. He is not a caterpillar and will never be a butterfly.

They did not believe in the little earthworm.

Susy and Rolly were about to give up hope then they met an ant with wings named Joseph. "How does an ant have wings?"

The flying ant told Rolly not to be sad or worried and to wait because he was a carpenter. He would take his wings off and give them to Rolly.

He said, "be patient Rolly; you'll get a surprise."

One day he got a present.

"Special delivery," said the snailman.

They went to the spider's house with the box.
Inside were real wings, not made of leaves.

The old spider smiled and helped them.

The spider spun his web and put the
ant's wings on the worm.

Rolly was very very happy.

The spider, ladybug, and worm went back to the tree. Rolly climbed a little bit higher this time.

When Rolly pushed away, he fell to the ground.

Plop!

The wings did not flap.

The mother bird is watching Rolly.

She sees his long wings.

Rolly said, "I am not giving up!"

He climbed back up in the tree. Pushed away.

He did not fall.

He was flying!

Rolly was in the air, then he looked to the sky and saw the mother bird holding onto his wings.

Oh no!

Was she going to eat him?

The mother bird held onto Rolly, and they went around and around in the clouds, way up in the tree, and in circles.

She put him back down on the ground.

She did not eat him.

Rolly said "Thank you. Why didn't you eat me?"

She said, "My babies will one day have strong wings and fly. But you are a worm who wants to fly. You can fly if you believe."

When Rolly went flying, others came to cheer, watch, and fly with him.

"Fly Rolly Fly," they shouted.

The worm would climb the tree, and they waited for him to push.

When he is about to fall, the mother bird catches him, and together they flew.

I hope you enjoyed the book and that it encourages you to share love and chase dreams.

For more inspirational books in the series, visit: www.vatsanabooks.com.

Printed in the USA
CPSIA information can be obtained
at www.ICGtesting.com
JSHW041540230923
48887JS00009BA/61